Quest for Clean Water

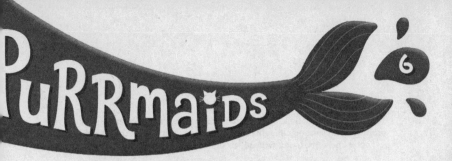

PuRRmaids

Quest for Clean Water

by Sudipta Bardhan-Quallen

illustrations by Vivien Wu

A STEPPING STONE BOOK™

Random House 🏠 New York

Text copyright © 2019 by Sudipta Bardhan-Quallen
Cover art copyright © 2019 by Andrew Farley
Interior illustrations copyright © 2019 by Vivien Wu

Visit us on the Web!
rhcbooks.com

Educators and librarians, for a variety of teaching tools, visit us at
RHTeachersLibrarians.com

Library of Congress Cataloging-in-Publication Data
Name: Bardhan-Quallen, Sudipta, author.
Title: Quest for clean water / Sudipta Bardhan-Quallen ;
illustrations by Vivien Wu.
Description: First edition. | New York: Random House, [2019]
Series: Purrmaids ; 6 | "A Stepping Stones Book."
Summary: Purrmaids Coral, Shelly, and Angel help clean up the ocean
as a school project and rescue the brother of their mermicorn friend, Sirena,
who is trapped by plastic soda rings.
Identifiers: LCCN 2018030317 | ISBN 978-0-525-64637-2 (trade pbk.) |
ISBN 978-0-525-64638-9 (lib. bdg.) | ISBN 978-0-525-64639-6 (ebook)
Subjects: | CYAC: Mermaids—Fiction. | Cats—Fiction. | Water—Pollution—
Fiction. | Ocean—Fiction. | Environmental protection—Fiction.
Classification: LCC PZ7.B25007 Que 2019 | DDC [Fic]—dc23

Printed in the United States of America
10 9 8 7 6 5 4 3 2
First Edition

This book has been officially leveled by using
the F&P Text Level Gradient™ Leveling System.

To Caroline,
my paw-some editor

1

Most days, Coral was early for sea school. But this morning, Coral was having one purr-oblem after another. First, she dropped her seaweed pancakes all over the ocean floor. She cleaned them up. But then she got a stain on her new top and had to change. Then she tried to put on her favorite bracelet. But she accidentally knocked a stack of snail mail *and* her bracelet behind a bookcase!

"Mama!" Coral shouted. "I can't reach my bracelet!" She frowned. "My arms are too short."

"I'm coming," Mama replied. She floated over and reached a paw behind the bookcase. "I can't quite get it," she said. "Help me move this out of the way."

Coral glanced at the clock on the wall. "I'm going to be late to school," she whined.

Coral loved many things about sea school. She loved being in the same class as her two best friends. She loved having the most fin-teresting teacher ever, Ms. Harbor, who made every day paw-sitively amazing.

"Do you want to go to sea school without it today?" Mama asked.

"No!" Coral yelped. She couldn't leave her bracelet behind! "You know Shelly,

Angel, and I wear our bracelets every day."

Shelly and Angel were Coral's best friends. They wore their matching friendship bracelets so that everyone in Kittentail Cove knew they were a team. Coral would rather be late than go without her bracelet—and she hated being late!

Coral moved to the far side of the bookcase. She and Mama pushed until it was a few inches away from the wall. "Do you see it?"

Coral gasped. "Yes, I do—and a lot more!" she exclaimed. She scooped up her bracelet and the snail mail. Then she picked up a sea-glass necklace, a book, a scallop shell from her last trip to Tortoiseshell Reef, and a half-eaten piece of Founder's Day candy. "I had no idea how much was back here!"

"Sometimes, if you look hard enough, you can find all sorts of unexpected things," Mama said.

Coral handed Mama the snail mail and said, "If I hurry, I can still get to sea school on time." She put her bracelet on her paw and reached for the doorknob.

Before Coral could open the door, Mama shouted, "Hold on a minute! There's something here for you." She held out an envelope.

Coral's eyes grew wide. She said, "Snail mail? For me?"

Mama nodded.

Coral had never gotten snail mail before. But there was no time to read a letter. "I'm running behind schedule," she said. "I'll take it with me." She stuffed the envelope in her bag and waved goodbye.

Coral hurried to Leondra's Square to

meet up with Shelly and Angel. When she saw them, she yelled, "I'm sorry I'm late! Let's hurry!" She zipped by her friends without even stopping.

Angel and Shelly looked at each other and shrugged. Usually, it was Coral who complained that the girls were swimming too fast. "You must be really worried about missing the bell!" Angel joked.

"Can't hear you!" Coral called. "You're too far behind me!"

It didn't take long for the girls to get to sea school. Coral's heart was pounding from swimming so fast. But, luckily, by the time the bell rang, Coral, Angel, and Shelly were at their desks in Room Eel-Twelve. All the other students in the class were there, too. The only one missing was the teacher!

"Where's Ms. Harbor?" Adrianna asked. "She's never late."

"She isn't under my desk," Baker said.

"She isn't under mine, either," Taylor said.

Angel rolled her eyes. "Of course, she isn't!" she said. She swam to the classroom door. "I'll check the hallway," she said, peeking left and right.

Coral spied a note on Ms. Harbor's

desk. She floated over to read it. Then she said, "I think we can stop looking." She motioned for everyone to come closer. "I don't think we'll find Ms. Harbor here. But I did find this." She read the note out loud.

Students of Eel-Twelve,
Please report to the schoolyard for this morning's lesson.
—Ms. Harbor

"Why does Ms. Harbor want us to go to the schoolyard?" Shelly asked.

"Maybe today's lesson is . . . RECESS!" Angel exclaimed.

"I'm really good at recess," Baker said.

"I don't even need a lesson!" Taylor added.

Coral giggled. "I don't think we're getting a lesson in recess," she said.

The purrmaids headed to the schoolyard. Ms. Harbor was there waiting to welcome them. "You found my note," she purred.

"Not right away," Angel said.

"We actually looked for you for a little while before Coral found your note," Cascade said.

"It's always fun to find something unexpected," Ms. Harbor said. "In fact, finding surprises is going to be our lesson today." She smiled at the class. "I'm sending you on a scavenger hunt!"

2

"A scavenger hunt?" Shelly asked. "What's that?"

"I know!" Coral said. "On a scavenger hunt, you get a list of things to find. The hunt is over when you've found everything on the list."

"Exactly!" Ms. Harbor purred.

"Are we searching the schoolyard?" Adrianna asked.

Ms. Harbor shook her head. "No, you'll

do your scavenger hunt after school. We're going to practice in the schoolyard. But first, we have to talk about what kinds of things you might find in the ocean." She motioned for the purrmaids to follow her. "All the creatures on this planet share the oceans in some way," she continued. "For example, sea birds, such as pelicans, use the ocean as a hunting ground for food. Humans use the ocean to travel across the world."

"And purrmaids use the ocean as a home," Angel said.

"Exactly!" Ms. Harbor exclaimed. "We all share a responsibility to keep the waters of the world clean and safe. But what is trash to one creature might be treasure to another." She pointed to something tucked near the bottom of a rock bench. "We've all seen bottle caps on the ocean floor. Sometimes humans throw them into the ocean, even though they really shouldn't."

"They're just garbage, right?" asked Umiko.

"They *are* trash to purrmaids," Ms. Harbor continued. "But some hermit crabs can reuse these bottle caps as homes."

"Really?" Coral asked.

Ms. Harbor nodded. "The bottle caps are lighter than seashells, so a crab who chooses one for a shell can move very quickly," Ms. Harbor explained. "We wish humans wouldn't let these litter the ocean. But it's nice that crabs are able to use them."

"So should we leave bottle caps alone?" Cascade asked.

"Make sure there's no crab first," Ms. Harbor replied. "If they're empty, throw them away properly."

The class floated to the school's small sea vegetable patch. Ms. Harbor pointed behind a sea lettuce and asked, "What do you all think of whale poop?"

"Gross!" groaned the class.

Ms. Harbor laughed. "I agree. But there are tiny ocean creatures who rely on whale poop for food. And humans actually use whale poop to make perfume."

"No way!" Baker exclaimed.

"They *want* to smell like whale poop?" Taylor groaned.

"Humans can be hard to understand,"

Ms. Harbor joked. "But that's a whole different lesson."

"We're not going to be hunting for whale poop, are we?" Shelly asked. She hated getting her paws dirty.

"Don't worry, Shelly," Ms. Harbor said. "Remember, since whale poop is reused as a source of food, it should remain wherever it is."

Shelly still looked a little seasick. "Let's talk about something else," she mumbled.

"I think there's something over here," Angel shouted. She reached under the sea-saw and grabbed a glass bottle and a metal soda can. "This bottle isn't garbage," she said. "We can make sea glass from this. And I love sea-glass jewelry!"

"The can isn't garbage, either," Adrianna said. "My uncle, the mayor, always says that purrmaids can recycle them and put them to good use."

"You're right," said Ms. Harbor.

The students spread out, looking for things they hadn't noticed before. Coral, Angel, and Shelly floated toward the waterslide. Shelly swam to the top and slipped down the slide. When she jumped off, she was holding something in her paws. "Look at these!" she shouted.

Ms. Harbor came over. "Pieces of a plastic fishing net and a few six-pack rings," she purred. "What should we do with them?"

Coral frowned. "We can't recycle any of that," she said. "They're definitely all trash."

Ms. Harbor nodded. "Most plastic things that end up in the ocean can't be reused or recycled. But they're not just litter. They can be dangerous. Many animals get tangled up in plastic garbage. Then they can't swim properly or open their mouths to eat."

"We don't want harmful things in our ocean," Baker said.

Taylor asked, "What can purrmaids do to help?"

"The most important thing is to make sure plastic gets removed from the ocean. It should always end up in garbage cans," Ms. Harbor said. "There's one more thing we can do to make these less dangerous." She extended one of her claws and used it to cut through the six-pack rings and fishing nets. "Now these can't get stuck around anything or anyone."

"That's easy to do," Shelly said.

"And it's a great excuse to get my claws out!" Adrianna joked.

"We have a few more minutes before we have to go back to Eel-Twelve," Ms. Harbor said. "Does anyone see anything else fin-teresting?"

Coral glanced around the schoolyard. She couldn't see any more bottles, cans, plastic bits, or even whale poop. She really wanted to find something special, just like Shelly and Angel had. "Maybe there's something near the sea-fan fence," she told her friends.

"I don't know," Angel said. "It looks purr-ty clean."

Coral shrugged. She checked the fence, from the tops of the sea fans to the sand on the ocean floor. She was about to give up when she spotted a flash of bright orange. She leaned in closer and gasped. "I found something!"

3

Coral pointed to the spiky orange thing on the far side of the fence. "Look, everyone!" she shouted.

Ms. Harbor floated next to Coral. Her eyes grew wide. "You found something fin-credible!" she said. "Can you get it for me?"

Coral nodded and reached for the orange spikes. But just like that morning with her bracelet, she was too small. "I can't reach it," she mumbled.

"I'll get it," Shelly purred. She picked up the orange thing and gave it to Ms. Harbor.

Coral tried not to frown.

"This is a basket starfish," Ms. Harbor said. "Its arms branch out many times 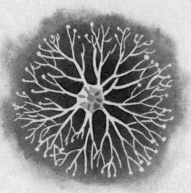 into twisty spikes, making it look like a basket." She gently placed the starfish back on the ground. "They are very, very rare. I've never seen one in Kittentail Cove." She grinned. "Coral made a real discovery!"

"What a paw-some way to finish the practice scavenger hunt," Angel whispered.

"It was almost as nice as when we *discovered* Sirena," Coral replied, smiling.

"But the basket starfish isn't something we have to keep secret," Shelly said.

Sirena was a mermicorn—a creature who was part mermaid and part unicorn. Coral, Shelly, and Angel had met her while they were exploring the nature reserve near the Kittentail Cove Science Center. Most purrmaids thought mermicorns were imaginary. But Coral and her friends knew they were real. Sirena was their first mermicorn friend!

Remembering Sirena made Coral smile as she went back to Eel-Twelve. When the students were settled, Ms. Harbor said, "I hope you all had fun outside."

"We did!" everyone replied.

Coral said, "I can't believe we found so much stuff in the schoolyard."

"I never noticed any of it before," Angel said.

"You can find a lot of unexpected things if you look hard enough," Ms. Harbor said. She floated to the board and held up her sea pen. "Outside, we found things that can be reused." She wrote *reused* on the board.

"Like bottle caps!" Baker shouted.

"And whale poop!" Taylor exclaimed.

Ms. Harbor nodded. "What else?" she asked.

Adrianna raised her paw. "There were things that can be recycled."

"Like glass bottles," Umiko said.

"And metal cans," Cascade said.

Ms. Harbor added *recycled* to the board.

Angel said, "There were also things that should be removed."

"Like all that plastic garbage," Shelly said.

Ms. Harbor wrote *removed* on the board. "Anything else?" she asked.

The students looked at each other. No one said anything.

"Think carefully," Ms. Harbor purred.

Coral had an idea. She raised her paw. "The basket starfish," she said. "It could be discovered."

"Purr-fect!" Ms. Harbor said. She added *discovered* to the board. "When you look carefully, you can find things in the ocean that can be reused, recycled, removed, or discovered," she said. "Tonight, I'd like you to get into groups and explore some part of Kittentail Cove. You could search your neighborhood, Meow Meadow, Leondra's Square, or anywhere else you want." She put a piece of paper on each student's desk. "Here's what you're searching for."

Coral read the instruction sheet.

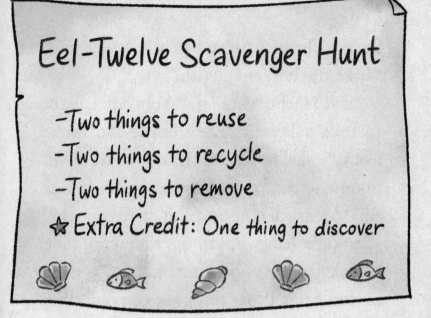

Eel-Twelve Scavenger Hunt

- Two things to reuse
- Two things to recycle
- Two things to remove

⭐ Extra Credit: One thing to discover

"Are we supposed to collect all these things?" Angel asked.

Coral scrunched her brow. "We can't collect all of it," she replied. She pointed to the instructions. "Someone might be using the reusable things. We shouldn't take those away."

"If we discover something, we might

have to leave it where it is," Angel said. "Like the basket starfish."

Ms. Harbor smiled. "You don't want to take a hermit crab's bottle-cap home away," she said. "You don't want to take a whale-poop feast away from our tiny ocean neighbors. But you probably shouldn't leave anything that could be recycled where you find it. It would be best to bring those things to our recycling centers."

"And we can't leave the garbage out in the ocean," Coral said. "Especially not the dangerous garbage. We have to make sure all of that gets cleaned up and thrown out!"

Shelly sighed. "I guess I can go hunting for garbage—if it keeps our ocean safe."

Ms. Harbor ducked behind her desk to grab something. "I'm going to give each group two bags. Use the green ones to collect anything for recycling. Use the red ones for trash."

"What do we take to prove we found things that we can't move?" Adrianna asked.

"You take notes!" Ms. Harbor exclaimed. "Come back tomorrow and describe what you found. Your notes will be all the proof I need."

4

When the school bell rang, Ms. Harbor purred, "The best thing you can do tonight is learn to pay attention to all the things around you."

"We can do that, right?" Shelly said.

Coral nodded. "As long as the three of us work together," she said, "I think we'll be just fine."

"Fine?" Angel said. "No, together we'll be paw-some!"

The purrmaids giggled and headed off to Coral's house. They swam to her kitchen for a snack. "We need to decide where to go for the scavenger hunt," Coral said.

"Can we eat first?" Shelly asked.

"I'm glad you girls are hungry," Papa said. He held out a tray of food.

"Sea cucumber sushi!" Coral shouted. "My favorite!"

"And shrimp salad!" Shelly added. "I love shrimp salad."

"And I love all of it!" Angel laughed.

The girls began to eat. Papa asked, "How was sea school today? Did you do anything fin-teresting?"

Coral's mouth was full so she mumbled, "Mm-hmm." She swallowed her mouthful and said, "Our homework is a scavenger hunt."

"That sounds fun!" Papa said. "What will you be hunting for?"

"I'll show you the instructions," Coral said. She opened her bag to find the sheet. But she'd been in such a hurry to pack up that the paper had gotten stuffed somewhere—and now she couldn't find it! "It should be here." She pawed through the bag. "What if I lost it?"

"It has to be in there," Shelly said. "I watched you put it away."

"Just dump out your bag," Angel suggested. "That's what I'd do."

Coral never liked making a mess. But she wanted to find the scavenger-hunt instructions quickly. So she spilled her bag out onto the kitchen table.

"Here it is!" Angel cried, holding up the sheet.

Coral reached for something else instead—her letter from that morning. "I forgot about this," she said.

"What is it?" Shelly asked.

"It's snail mail," Coral said. "For me."

"That's so exciting!" Angel exclaimed. "I've never gotten snail mail addressed to me."

"Me neither," Shelly added.

Coral looked at the envelope. Her name was written clearly on the front. She turned it around to see who sent it.

Sirena Cheval
Seadragon Bay

"It's from Sirena!" Coral squealed. She held the envelope out for her friends to see.

"Sirena?" Angel asked. "From Siren Island?"

"It does say Seadragon Bay," Shelly said. "It must be her."

"We were just talking about her today," Coral said. "I wonder why she wrote to me."

"Read it!" Shelly and Angel said together.

Dear Coral,

My family and I are camping in Ponyfish Grotto on the edge of Tortoiseshell Reef this week. I know that is close to Kittentail Cove. I thought maybe you could visit me there.

Love,
Sirena

P.S. I sent the same invitation to Angel and Shelly. I hope they can come, too!

"I would love to see Sirena again!" Shelly said. Angel nodded.

Coral frowned. "I want to see her again, too," she said. "But when we went to Tortoiseshell Reef, we got lost."

"That's one way to look at it," Angel replied. "But you could also say that the last time we went to Tortoiseshell Reef, we found a shipwreck, sunken treasure, and a new friend!"

Coral sighed. Angel was right. That trip really was paw-some. But it was also a little scary! "What about our homework?" Coral asked. "We need to do our scavenger hunt. We might not have enough time to finish that *and* go see Sirena."

Shelly scowled. "Our homework does come first," she said.

Angel crossed her paws and tapped her tail on the ground. Suddenly, she exclaimed, "I have a great idea! We can head toward Tortoiseshell Reef to see Sirena. On the way, we can look for the things in the scavenger hunt."

5

"Come on, Coral," Shelly said.

"It'll be an exciting adventure!" Angel said.

Coral gulped. Angel always loved an adventure. Shelly did, too—as long as it wasn't too messy. Coral would be fine keeping things a little boring. That was safer—and it didn't involve breaking any rules. "Can't we find something a little less exciting?" she asked. "And a little less adventurous?"

Angel rolled her eyes. "Oh, Coral," she said. "Don't be such a scaredy cat!"

"I'm not scared!" Coral replied. "It's just that . . . I don't even know where Ponyfish Grotto is. Do you?" When her friends shook their heads, she asked, "Then how will we find Sirena?"

"Who's Sirena?" Papa asked. "Is she the friend you met at the Kittentail Cove Science Center?"

Coral nodded. She told her parents all about Sirena after their visit to the Science Center. The only thing she had left out was that Sirena was a mermicorn.

Sirena said that mermicorns liked to stay out of sight. Staying hidden was how they kept themselves safe. That's why

Coral, Shelly, and Angel had decided not to tell anyone in Kittentail Cove how to find Sirena or the mermicorn town of Seadragon Bay. They wanted the mermicorns to decide whether or not they wanted to meet any other purrmaids.

"Sirena lives far away, but her family is camping in Ponyfish Grotto this week," Shelly said. "We were trying to decide whether to go see them."

"We can even get our homework done on our way there," Angel said.

"But we don't know where Ponyfish Grotto is," Coral said. "So I don't know if we should go."

"I can tell you how to get there," Papa said. "I used to go camping in Tortoiseshell Reef when I was your age. On the edge of the reef, the rocks and coral form a deep tunnel. If you swim through the tunnel, you'll find a geyser. My friends and I used to swim into the geyser and get flipped through the water."

"We've been there!" Coral exclaimed.

"And we let the geyser spin us all around, too!" Angel added. "At least, I did."

"Fin-tastic!" Papa said. "Then you know how to get to Ponyfish Grotto."

Coral scratched her head. A grotto was a type of cave. "I definitely remember the tunnel," she said. "But I don't remember a cave anywhere nearby."

"That's because there isn't a cave," Papa said. "Ponyfish Grotto got its name long ago, before I was born. Maybe it was a real grotto once. But unless there's a secret entrance, now it's just what we call the giant rocks around the tunnel."

"So we know exactly how to get there,"

Shelly said. "We don't have to worry about getting lost."

"Please, Coral," Angel begged. "You know we can find Ponyfish Grotto and get our homework done, as long as we work together."

Coral bit her lip. She couldn't let her best friends down. "Do we have the recycling bag and the trash bag?" she asked.

"Yes!" Angel replied. She tossed the red bag over her shoulder and gave the green one to Coral.

"And the instruction sheet?" Coral asked.

Shelly held the page up. "Got it!" she cried. "And I have a notebook for writing things down."

"Let's go, then," Coral said. "We've got a lot to do!"

"Have a paw-some time, girls," Papa purred, waving goodbye.

The purrmaids hurried to the South Canary Current. It carried them from the entrance of Kittentail Cove straight to Tortoiseshell Reef. When the girls arrived, they stopped for a moment to gaze all around. They were surrounded by elkhorns and sea fans, schools of fish and herds of sea horses.

But today, Coral didn't just see the natural beauty of the reef. She started to notice other things.

There was a plastic bag floating in the water like a cloud. There were two metal cans tucked under reef rocks. There were plastic straws tangled in patches of sea grass. Almost everywhere she looked, Coral saw something that didn't belong in the ocean.

"It's just like the schoolyard," Shelly purred. "There's so much stuff I never paid attention to before."

"The reef is so beautiful," Angel said. "I guess it's easy to ignore the things that aren't so purr-ty."

"At least this makes it easier to finish our homework," Coral said. "Are you ready to start?"

The girls nodded. Angel took out the instructions. "We need to find two things to reuse, two things to recycle, two things to remove, and one thing to discover," she said.

"We have to find one other thing, too," Coral said. *"A mermicorn!"*

Angel and Shelly laughed. "You're right, Coral," Angel said.

"Let's not waste any more time," Shelly said.

Coral nodded. "Let's dive in to this assignment!"

6

"What do you want to collect first?" Coral asked her friends.

"Well, I'd like to find Sirena," Angel said. "But we have to get to the other side of Tortoiseshell Reef to reach Ponyfish Grotto."

"We might as well find the things on the scavenger-hunt list on the way," Shelly said.

Coral purred, "We should definitely

remove all the dangerous garbage we see. Things like fishing nets could cause so much harm. We don't want to leave them behind. So maybe we should start with that?"

"Coral is right," Angel said. "I'm starting by removing these." She floated down to the ocean floor and scooped up some bottle caps. But then she shrieked, "EEEEEEEK!"

"What's wrong?" Shelly asked. She and Coral rushed to Angel's side.

"I don't think all of these are garbage," Angel said. She showed the bottle caps to the other girls. Little crab legs were poking out of them!

"You found hermit crabs!" Coral exclaimed.

Angel said, "I'm going to leave these little guys here."

"Let's write this down as a reusable thing," Shelly suggested.

"Good idea," Coral said.

While Angel gently put the crabs back in the sand, Coral looked all around. A sea turtle swam toward a huge sea fan. Coral recognized it from their last trip to the reef. She knew they had to swim that way to reach the reef's edge. But this time, she saw something else. There was a plastic six-pack ring wrapped around the sea fan's fronds.

Coral swam to the sea fan. "Look over here," she said. She pulled the plastic off.

"Is that a six-pack ring?" Shelly asked.

"It is," Coral replied. She sliced the rings open with her claw. "I'm removing this garbage right away."

"Speaking of garbage," Shelly said, "how about these?" She picked up a pawful of plastic straws. "There are a lot of straws stuck in the sea grass. Animals could eat them by mistake."

Angel held the red trash bag open. "Toss them in here," she said.

The girls searched for more straws in the sea-grass beds. Coral picked up a bunch and then looked for Angel and the trash bag. That's when she saw the plastic bag from before. It was still floating through the water. It looked like a jelly-fish in the sunlight.

Maybe that's why the sea turtle snapped the bag up in its jaws!

"Shelly! Angel!" Coral shouted. "Come quickly!" She pointed to the turtle. "We have to help!"

Coral raced toward the sea turtle. But the turtle didn't want to be caught! He clenched the plastic bag tightly and swam off.

Most of the time, sea turtles moved very slowly. When they wanted to, though, they could swim as fast as dolphins! It was hard for the quickest purrmaids to keep up with a sea turtle at full speed. Coral knew that, and she knew she wasn't the fastest purrmaid in the ocean. But with the turtle in danger, she wasn't giving up!

Luckily, Coral wasn't alone. Angel and

Shelly were there to help. Angel swam toward the turtle from the left. Shelly swam from the right. The turtle zigged one way and then zagged another. He was so busy trying to keep away from Shelly and Angel that he didn't notice Coral—until she pulled the plastic bag out of his mouth! "Got it!" she exclaimed.

The turtle didn't look happy to lose his snack. But Coral had a plan. She scooped up a sea cucumber from the sand. She held the plastic bag behind her back with one paw and offered the turtle the sea cucumber with the other. "Come on, Mr. Turtle," she purred. "Sea cucumbers taste better than plastic bags, I purr-omise."

The turtle sniffed at the sea cucumber. He took one small bite and then another. Soon, he snapped up the whole thing and swam away.

"Coral!" Shelly exclaimed. "You saved him!"

7

Coral smiled. "You don't get to be a sea turtle superhero every day," she said. "But I couldn't have done it without the two of you."

"We do make a purr-fect team," Shelly said.

"You even found something else to remove from the reef," Angel said.

"That makes three—and we only needed two!" Shelly said.

"I'm glad we cleaned it up, though," Coral said.

The other girls nodded, and Coral pointed toward Ponyfish Grotto. "Let's keep going," she said. "Maybe we can save someone else today!"

The purrmaids swam through more of Tortoiseshell Reef. Like before, they saw many things that weren't supposed to be in the ocean. Shelly found metal soda cans and threw them into the green recycling bag. Angel spied some glass bottles and tossed those in, too. "These can be reused as sea glass," Angel said. "But they could be recycled, too."

"We found everything on the scavenger-hunt list, but we haven't discovered anything," Shelly said.

"Let's keep looking," Coral said. She swung the green bag onto her shoulder.

It was really full—and really heavy. She struggled to pull it and keep up with Shelly and Angel.

Angel noticed that Coral was falling behind. "Let's trade," she said. "That bag is too heavy for someone your size."

Angel held out the red bag. But Coral didn't take it. *I hate being the smallest one,* she thought. "I'll be fine," Coral said. She tried to keep swimming. But after a minute, she had to let the bag go. She sighed. "Maybe I *am* too little to carry this." She stared down at her tail. "I'm too little for everything."

Angel patted her friend's shoulder. "We think you're paw-some just the way you are," she said.

Shelly added, "There's nothing wrong with letting your friends help."

Coral shrugged and took the red bag. Even though it was lighter, she swam just a little bit slower.

Soon, the girls were close to the edge of the reef. They saw the giant rocks that Papa said marked Ponyfish Grotto. Coral always thought the rocks were a little scary—there were so many gaps and cracks that could be hiding an octopus or an eel. But today, they looked scarier than usual. Something was blocking the sunlight, and there were more shadows than ever. "It's so dark," Coral said.

Shelly pointed to the ocean above the rocks. "The kelp has grown a lot since the last time we were here."

"The fronds reach almost to the surface," Coral said. "And they're all tangled

up. Only a few beams of sunlight can shine down through the kelp."

The girls looked for their mermicorn friend. "Do you see Sirena?" Angel asked.

Shelly and Coral shook their heads. "She said she'd be here with her family," Shelly said. "I guess that means we should find a herd of mermicorns."

"I have a question," Angel said. "If mermicorns come to Tortoiseshell Reef to go camping, then why haven't other purrmaids seen them before?"

Coral scratched her head. "I don't think Sirena will just be swimming out in the open," she said. "Remember, she said mermicorns like to keep to the shadows."

"You're right," Shelly said.

"And," Coral continued, "this scavenger hunt has shown us that there are a lot of things in the ocean that you never see—unless you go looking for them."

Angel nodded. "So purrmaids have never seen mermicorns in Tortoiseshell Reef because they've never looked for them," she said.

"Well, we're looking," Shelly said. "So I hope we find her soon!"

"The only thing left for our homework is something to discover," Angel said. "Maybe Sirena can be our discovery—if she's okay with us telling Kittentail Cove about mermicorns."

Coral shrugged. "It's her decision."

"Of course!" Angel said. "Let's find her and ask."

Coral looked all around. She didn't see any horns or hooves. She didn't see any rainbow tails or flowing manes. But she did see the rock-and-coral tunnel. It was mermicorn-sized—and very shadowy. "Maybe we should check there for Sirena first," she said, pointing. "It looks like it might be a good place to hide."

The purrmaids floated closer to the entrance of the tunnel. They peeked inside. "It's longer than I remember," Angel whispered. "Darker, too."

Coral gulped. It was never good when

Angel looked scared. "Maybe this isn't a good idea," she said.

Shelly looked nervous, too. But she shook her head. "We've been all over Tortoiseshell Reef," she said. "We haven't seen a trace of Sirena all afternoon. I think Coral was right when she said the mermicorns would probably be hiding."

"Except for that tangle of kelp, this is the best hiding spot I've seen all day," Angel added.

Coral looked down the tunnel again. She thought, *Why do we always end up in the spooky places?* But she squared her shoulders and turned to her friends. "We'll take a quick look," she said. "And we'll stick together."

The girls entered the tunnel. "It's really hard to see," Shelly said.

"I swam through too quickly last time

to notice how little light there is," Angel said.

"Follow me," Coral purred. She moved slowly, touching the wall as she went. Suddenly, she shrieked, "I can't believe it!"

"What?" Shelly asked.

It was so dark it looked like the wall of the tunnel was right there. But when Coral reached out to touch the wall, there was actually a hole in the side of the tunnel. "I think I found . . . a secret entrance!"

8

"What do you mean?" Angel asked. "I don't see anything."

"It's hard to see because there's no light," Coral replied. "But there's no wall here." She floated forward. And she was right! "There's another tunnel!"

"Should we explore?" Shelly asked.

"That's what we're here to do!" Coral laughed. She craned her neck. The water in the distance was brighter, like it was open to sunlight. "I think I see the end of the tunnel."

"Don't leave us behind," Angel said. She and Shelly hurried to catch up to Coral. "We all do this together."

The purrmaids used their paws to feel for the walls of the secret tunnel. They reached the end and swam out slowly.

The girls knew the other tunnel led to a geyser. But this one took them to a large cave. The rock walls reached the surface of the ocean. But it wasn't dark because sunlight filtered in through openings at the top.

"This looks almost exactly like Tortoiseshell Reef," Coral said.

"That's because it's a part of Tortoiseshell Reef," someone said.

Coral thought she recognized the voice. But she spun around quickly to make sure.

"Sirena!" she cried. "We've been trying to find you. But you found us!"

"We found each other!" Sirena giggled. She hugged each of her purrmaid friends. "I'm so happy you came to see me. Welcome to Ponyfish Grotto!"

Coral's eyes grew wide. "*This* is Pony-fish Grotto?" she asked.

"There are no other caves in Tortoise-shell Reef," Sirena said.

"We didn't even know *this* cave was here!" Shelly said.

"Purrmaids think Ponyfish Grotto is the area outside the tunnel," Angel added.

Sirena looked confused. "Then how did you find me?" she asked.

"We discovered the entrance to the grotto!" Coral laughed. "We've been searching for things all afternoon. Our homework tonight was a scavenger hunt," she said. "Mermicorns weren't on the list, but we looked for you anyway."

"I'm glad you did," Sirena replied. "I want to introduce you to my parents. And to my little brother, Clyde. He's just a foal. He can be annoying, but he's really cute."

"I understand." Coral giggled. "I have a little brother, too." She put a paw around Sirena's waist and squeezed. "It's paw-some to see you again!"

Just then, someone shouted, "Get away from my daughter!"

The girls spun around. A mermicorn was speeding toward them. Her red-and-gold mane flowed behind her, and her coppery scales glistened in the light. Coral would have thought she was beautiful—if she didn't look so scared! "Please don't hurt her," the mermicorn cried.

Sirena darted in front of the purrmaids. "Mom!" she yelled. "No one is hurting me!"

"I saw her grab you!" the mermicorn

replied. She pulled Sirena away from the purrmaids. "I was so frightened!"

"She's afraid of *Coral*?" Angel whispered. "No one's afraid of Coral!"

"We were just talking, Mom," Sirena said. "These are my friends Coral, Shelly, and Angel. They helped me get home to Seadragon Bay when I was lost. Girls, this is my mother, Mrs. Cheval."

Coral, Angel, and Shelly waved at Sirena's mother. "Sirena did tell us that purrmaids helped her get home," Mrs. Cheval said. "But we weren't sure what she saw." She shrugged. "I always thought creatures who are half-cat and half-mermaid were just make-believe."

Coral grinned. "That's what we used to think about mermicorns!"

Mrs. Cheval smiled. "I owe you girls an apology," she said. "I'm sorry I thought you were hurting my daughter. It's just that mermicorns have to be so careful. We usually stay hidden away from other sea creatures. There are so many dangers in the ocean."

The purrmaids nodded. Angel said, "Sirena told us that when we met."

"That's why we didn't tell anyone else

in Kittentail Cove about Seadragon Bay," Coral said.

"We didn't even tell them about meeting a mermicorn," Shelly said.

"That's really kind," Mrs. Cheval said. "Sirena has very good friends. I'm glad you found each other."

"Mom," Sirena said, "I want my friends to meet Dad and Clyde. Where are they?"

Mrs. Cheval thought for a moment. "They went out earlier to collect silver tower shells," she said.

"I love silver tower shells!" Sirena exclaimed. "They're fin-tastic. They look just like mermicorn horns. But they are very rare." She turned to her mother. "How many did Dad and Clyde bring back?"

"I don't know if they *are* back," Mrs. Cheval said. She frowned. "I hope nothing happened to them." She swam out into the tunnels with Sirena on her tail. The purrmaids left their bags against the grotto wall and followed the mermicorns. Out in Tortoiseshell Reef, Mrs. Cheval asked, "Do you see any mermicorns?"

Sirena, Shelly, and Angel said no. Coral didn't see anything, either—but she thought she might have heard something. "Quiet!" she cried. "I think someone is shouting."

9

Coral held up a paw for silence just like Ms. Harbor did at sea school. After a moment, Angel whispered, "I hear it, too."

"It sounds like it's coming from that kelp," Coral said. She pointed to the seaweed they'd noticed earlier.

"Let's go check it out," Shelly said.

But Mrs. Cheval held the girls back.

"There could be anything in there!" she said. "What if it's dangerous?"

Whoever was stuck in the kelp shouted again. But this time, he was louder. "Help!" he cried.

Someone else yelled, "I'm trying, son!"

"That sounds like Clyde and Dad!" Sirena cried. "We have to go to them!"

This time, Mrs. Cheval nodded. The group raced toward the kelp tangle. It was so overgrown that it looked like a solid wall.

As they got closer, Coral noticed something else. There were plastic straws, bags, and nets twisted into the seaweed. "Look at all this garbage," she said.

"I never noticed any of this stuff before," Angel said.

"Me neither," Shelly said.

"Can we clean up later?" Sirena asked. She was close to tears. "I want to find my family!"

"Of course," Coral purred. "That's what we're here for."

The yelling started again. The group followed the sound and swam around the tangle of seaweed. When they turned the corner, they saw a flowing silver mane. A mermicorn floated near the kelp, pushing at it with his hooves. "Dad!" Sirena exclaimed.

Sirena and Mrs. Cheval darted toward the silver-maned mermicorn. They pulled him into a hug. "Where have you been?" Sirena asked.

"And where is our son?" Mrs. Cheval asked.

Mr. Cheval was about to answer when he noticed the purrmaids. He looked

just as scared as Mrs. Cheval had been.
"Watch out!" he warned. His nostrils
flared and he snorted. "I'll try to chase
them away!"

"No, Dad!" Sirena yelled. "We don't
have time to explain right now. Those are
purrmaids. They're my friends."

"We're only here to help," Coral said.

Mr. Cheval looked at his daughter and
then at the purrmaids. Before he could

say anything, the voice behind the kelp shouted, "Help me! I'm trapped."

"Please just trust me, Dad," Sirena said. "We have to help Clyde now!"

Mr. Cheval nodded. "You're right," he neighed. He pointed to the kelp tangle. "Clyde is behind this seaweed. He slipped in somehow, and now he can't get out. I've been looking for a way to reach him. But I can't find a hole big enough for me to fit!"

"Clyde was able to swim in," Coral said. "That means there has to be a way. Look for a secret entrance!"

The purrmaids and mermicorns examined the seaweed closely. There were a few spots where a paw or a hoof could slide in. But no one could find the passage that Clyde must have used.

Out of the corner of her eye, Coral saw some moving bottle caps near her tail. *More hermit crabs,* she thought. The crabs climbed up a frond of seaweed and then darted into the tangle. Then Coral saw more bottle-cap crabs near the top of the kelp tangle. They scrambled down the seaweed and darted inside as well—but in a different spot than the crabs from below.

Coral swam closer. Then she gasped. "I found it!"

Just like the tunnel to Ponyfish Grotto, the shadows in the seaweed made it look solid. But there was an opening leading to a narrow tunnel. "I think this is the way Clyde went," Coral said.

Everyone gathered around Coral. "You might be right," Sirena said. She began to swim into the tunnel. But only her head and neck fit in the hole. "I'm too big!"

"Then your father and I will never fit," Mrs. Cheval whinnied.

"Sirena? Is that you?" Clyde's voice called. It was louder than before.

We must be really close, Coral thought.

Angel studied the opening. "This is too small for all of you," she said. "Only a really small mermicorn could fit."

"Or maybe a purrmaid?" Coral suggested.

"You're closer to Clyde's size than we are," Mrs. Cheval said.

"One of us can try to reach him," Shelly said.

"I'll do it!" Angel offered. She tried to swim into the hole. She got farther than Sirena. But then she stopped. "It's

starting to get really tight. I hope I don't get stuck."

Coral gulped. Angel was smaller than Sirena. *But I'm even smaller than Angel,* she thought. She knew which purrmaid had the best chance of getting through the kelp. She shouted, "Angel, stop!" She took a deep breath. "Let me try. I'm the smallest one here. If anyone can get to Clyde, it'll be me."

10

Coral peeked into the hole in the kelp. There were more crabs scurrying into the opening. There were fish swimming inside, too. But more important, there were ocean creatures swimming *out* of the tunnel. Coral thought, *If they can do it, so can I!*

"We believe in you, Coral," Shelly whispered.

"You've already saved one creature

today," Angel added. "We know you can do it again."

Coral smiled at her friends and purred, "I'll be right back!" It sounded braver than she was feeling. But she knew she had to try to help Clyde. She entered the tunnel and called, "I'm coming to get you, Clyde!"

"Who are you?" Clyde replied. "Where's my family?"

Coral listened to Clyde's voice. It was even louder. She was getting closer. "I'm Coral," she said. "Your family is outside. They were too big to reach you, so they sent me."

It was getting very dark in the tunnel. Coral felt her way through. Suddenly, her paw caught on something. "Eek!" she squealed.

"Are you all right?" Clyde yelled.

"I think so," Coral answered. She brought her paw close to her face. There was a fishing net twisted around it. "More garbage," she muttered. "It's everywhere." She ripped the net open with her claws and held onto the pieces. "Now no one else will get caught on this."

"Are you still coming for me, Coral?" Clyde asked.

"Yes, I am!" Coral shouted. "I can hear you really well now. I think I'm almost there!"

The tunnel was getting narrower. But Coral squeezed through toward Clyde's voice. Finally, she reached a hollow part inside the kelp tangle. That's where she found Clyde!

"I'm here!" Coral called.

Clyde's eyes grew wide. "You—you're

a . . . purrmaid!" he stammered. "Sirena told me about you!"

Coral grinned. "Sirena is my friend. That's why I'm here to get you out!"

Clyde frowned. "I'm stuck," he said. "I can't swim like this."

It was brighter in the hollow than in the tunnel, but Coral still had to swim closer to see. When she did, she gasped. There were plastic six-pack rings and fishing nets looped and knotted around Clyde's hooves and tail. "What happened?" she asked.

Clyde shrugged. "I was out with my dad collecting tower shells. That's when I discovered the tunnel in the kelp. I thought it would be an adventure! But when I swam inside, I got all these things on me. At first, it was fine. But the farther I went, the more stuff got stuck. By the time I got here, I was in a twisted, knotted mess!" he moaned. He lowered his head. "I don't have anything to cut through the plastic. I can't get myself free."

"But I can do it!" Coral laughed. She flashed Clyde her claws. "I know what to do!"

It took Coral a while to cut every piece of plastic that was tangled around Clyde. As soon as she was done, Clyde popped up and twirled in the water. "I'm free! Thank you!" he exclaimed.

Coral carefully gathered all the plastic. She wanted to make sure she could throw it away properly later. Then she turned to Clyde. "There's still a lot of trash in the tunnel. Be careful when you're swimming out. Go slowly so you don't get too tangled up," she said. "Let's get you back to your family!"

Clyde nodded and followed Coral. The two moved carefully toward the open ocean.

As soon as Angel and Shelly saw

Coral's face poking through the seaweed, they swam to her. They grabbed her paws and pulled her out. "Coral!" Shelly said. "We were worried!"

Before Coral could say anything, Clyde wriggled out of the kelp. The mermicorns rushed over. They wrapped Clyde in a group hug. "Oh, Clyde," Mrs. Cheval whinnied. "You're safe!"

Sirena let go of her family. "You saved him," she said to Coral, hugging her friend.

"Yeah, Coral," Angel said. "You're a sea turtle superhero *and* a mermicorn superhero!"

"I think she's just an ocean superhero," Shelly said.

Coral felt her face growing hot. "I'm glad I was small enough to help," she said.

"And *I'm* glad you were brave enough," Sirena said.

Mr. and Mrs. Cheval gave each purrmaid a hug. "We're lucky that you three were here," Mr. Cheval said. "Mermicorns can't cut through plastic the way you can."

"We try to keep the ocean clean so we don't get stuck like Clyde did," Mrs. Cheval added. "You girls helped do that today."

Clyde swam up to Coral. "I want to thank you," he said. "And I want you to have these." He held something out to her.

"Are these silver tower shells?" Coral asked.

Clyde nodded. "They're really hard to find. I want you to have these three for saving me."

Coral took the shells and held them for Angel and Shelly to see. They looked like purr-fect silver models of Sirena's horn.

"Since these shells are rare, can they count as our discovery?" Shelly asked. "That is the only part of the scavenger hunt we haven't finished."

Coral scratched her head. "They *are* rare. But we didn't really discover them," she said.

"But you did discover the mermicorns who discovered them!" Sirena said.

"I think that counts!" Angel laughed.

Suddenly, Coral had an idea. "You know what else?" she asked. "These shells will be purr-fect for our friendship bracelets."

"You're right!" Angel said.

"We can attach them as soon as we get back to Kittentail Cove," Shelly said.

"That way we'll always remember this scavenger hunt," Angel said.

"What a day!" Coral exclaimed. "New discoveries, secret entrances, saving lives . . . and we even finished all of our homework!"

New friends. New...

Find a new series...

ISADORA MOON

MAGIC ON THE M...

ISADORA MOON
Goes to School

Harriet Muncaster

**For ballerina
and fairy and
vampire lovers**

MAGIC ON THE MAP
LET'S MOOOVE!

COURTNEY SHEINMEL
& BIANCA TURETSKY

For adventurers

JULIE SYKES

**For unicorn
lovers**

PUPPY PIRATES

PURRMAIDS

BALLPARK Mysteries

PUPPY PIRATES
Stowaway!

Erin Soderberg

For dog lovers

PURRMAIDS
The Scaredy Cat

**For mermaid
and cat
lovers**

BALLPARK Mysteries SUPER SPECIAL #1
THE WORLD SERIES CURSE

David A. Kelly

**For
sports
fans**

31901064902804